The
Three Princes
of Serendip

New Tellings of Old Tales
for Everyone

The
Three Princes
of Serendip

New Tellings of Old Tales
for Everyone

told by **Rodaan Al Galidi**   illustrated by **Geertje Aalders**
translated by **Laura Watkinson**

CANDLEWICK PRESS

A Note from the Gatherer of Tales

Dear eyes that read this book,
  dear warm hands that hold it,

Stories are the best travelers and the most successful migrants that have ever existed on our beautiful planet. If you take cheese from the Netherlands to Iraq, people there might say, "That's Dutch cheese." If I take wooden shoes to Suriname, the locals might say, "Hey, look! Dutch clogs!"

However, a tale changes when it travels from the Netherlands to Iraq or to Suriname. It becomes an Iraqi tale or a Surinamese one, because stories do not believe in borders or countries or languages or identity or culture. Stories belong to everyone and are for everyone.

So in this collection, you will find folk tales that have traveled a long way. Some of them were originally Russian, but when I heard them in Iraq, they had become Iraqi, and Ivan had turned into Murat. Other stories may come from Germany, Turkey, or other countries without my ever realizing they were not from Iraq.

Like a sort of gatherer of tales, I went in search of the most beautiful stories from my childhood, from literature, from history, and I tried to rewrite them in my own style. So these are not my own stories, but stories that belong to everyone.

I wish you lots of pleasure reading this book, and I hope that you will give my stories a chance to become stories from wherever it is that you live. Feel free to change the names or to choose other flowers, waters, windows, or doors. Because, as I said: stories are the best migrants and the finest travelers. Let these stories become your own.

Rodaan Al Galidi

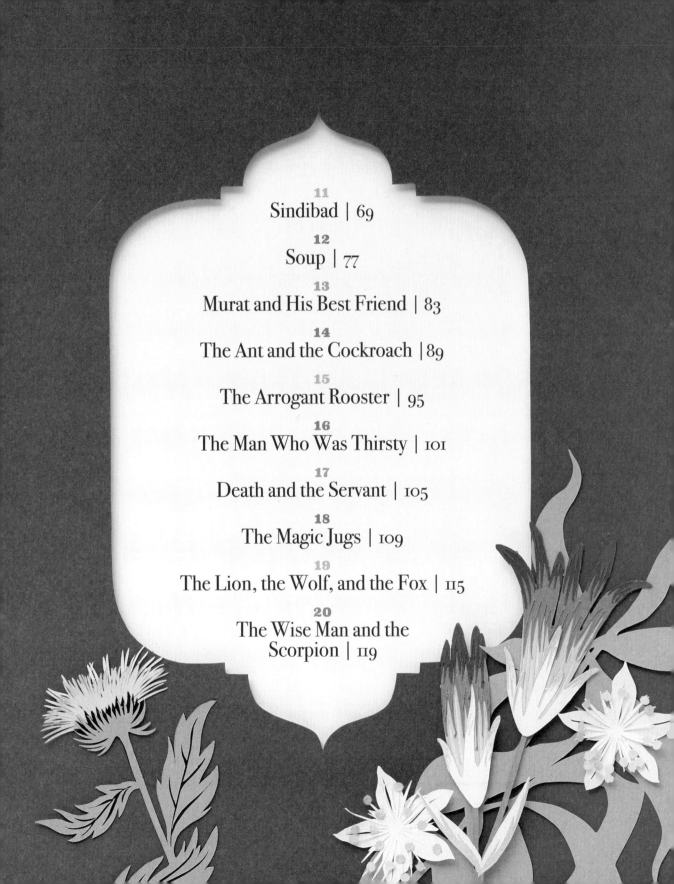

Jordion

1

There was once a mighty man who owned the whole kingdom. His name was Niron. He had soldiers, money, buildings, jails, and many, many other things. In fact, everything in the country belonged to him.

Far from the palace, somewhere in the desert, there lived a man who had nothing. His name was Jordion. Jordion was the only person in the country who was not afraid of Niron.

One day, Niron called for his bravest soldier, Nadi. "Listen, Nadi," he said. "Everyone in the country obeys me. Everyone admires me, and everyone fears me. Everyone except for Jordion, that is. So I command you to go to the desert and kill him."

Nadi bowed to Niron, took his horse and his sword, and set out for the desert, where Jordion lived.

On the way there, however, Nadi had plenty of time to think. *I don't want to kill Jordion,* he thought. *He has not done anything wrong, not to me and not to Niron. He does not harm anyone. He lives in the desert, owns nothing, and longs for nothing. But what can I do? I am a soldier. I must obey the king and carry out his orders.*

The whole journey his heart said to him: "Don't do it. You do not have to listen if Niron asks you to do something that is not good." And the whole journey his head said: "You have no choice. You must obey, or Niron will be furious with you—and you will not survive his rage."

Nadi traveled through the desert for days until he saw a thin man who was dressed in a white piece of cloth and sitting by a small date palm tree.

Found him! thought Nadi. *Oh, he has such a kind face! He is wearing an old robe, and he does not even have sandals for his feet. He lives here peacefully, with little to eat and drink, and he does no one any harm. But I have been ordered to kill him. I have no choice. I will do it quickly so that he does not realize what I am planning. Then it will be less painful for him.*

Having hidden his sword under his clothes, Nadi approached Jordion and gave him a friendly smile.

"My dear Jordion, how are you today?"

Jordion looked into Nadi's eyes, saw the uncertainty there, and knew at once that the soldier was not saying what he was thinking.

"Nadi, you are a soldier. You do not do what you want, but what others want you to do. I know you have not

traveled all this way just to say hello. No, you were sent by Niron. Have you come to kill me? Then please do it quickly. I am not afraid of death, because I have never done anything wrong."

"Aha, so you know why I have come," Nadi replied, drawing his sword. "That makes it easier. But before I kill you, you may say a prayer."

"What should I pray for?" asked Jordion.

"Pray for me. Pray for the animals. Pray for the birds. Pray for whatever you find beautiful."

"But Nadi," said Jordion, "if I pray for what I find beautiful, I will be praying for a good while. Hours, days, weeks, months, years, maybe even centuries."

"And what if you are?" said Nadi. "I am a man of my word. I have said that you may pray, and I shall wait until you have finished."

Jordion kneeled and began to pray. He prayed for everything he found beautiful. For the trees, which provide fruit without taking anything. For the springs, which bring water. For the rivers, which provide a bed for the water. For the birds, which fill the sky with their singing and their beautiful colors. For the flowers, which give the world their scent. For the air, which is everywhere and for everyone. For the light, for the stars, for the mountains, and for the sea.

He prayed for an hour, a day, a week, a month, a year.

He prayed for centuries and centuries. And because of the love with which Jordion prayed, the little date palm tree grew and began to give fruit. More palm trees grew from the stones of those dates, until a forest sprang up. Birds made nests in the trees and laid their eggs. Springs flowed with water for foxes and deer to drink, and a new world was born.

And Nadi? He stood waiting beside Jordion. His clothes rotted away, his skin grew old and wrinkled, and his sword rusted, but he kept his word, and he waited and he waited. 🪲

— 2 —

The Partridge and the Turtles

There was once an island where only turtles lived. They were happy on the island and had been so for years because it was full of fruit trees and plants they could eat. The turtles went out all day long, looking for food, and in the evening they met up again in the spot where they lived. But one day something different happened. Out of nowhere, a partridge landed on their island. What a miracle! *Such wondrous beauty!* thought the turtles. They had never seen anything so magnificent before.

The partridge had become hot and tired when flying over the great ocean and had flown down to the dot of green far below. That dot turned out to be the turtles' island.

The turtles were thankful for this very fine visitor, and they gave the partridge a warm and friendly welcome. The partridge soon felt so at home among the turtles that he decided to stay. They grew fond of one another, the partridge and the turtles. During the daytime the partridge flew off to look for food, and in the evening he returned to sleep with the turtles.

After some time, the turtles began to miss the partridge during the daytime. They saw him only at night, and they said to one another: "Oh, how can we live without seeing him? He is the most beautiful thing on our island, and whenever he leaves, we miss his beauty. Our island is already beautiful, but he makes it even more so. We would love for him to stay with us forever. And for him not to be here only when it is dark. What can we do to keep him here? Whatever will we do if he leaves one day and we never see him again?"

"Sisters," said one of the turtles, who believed she was smarter than the rest, "all we need to do is ask him to stay. Staying is a sign of love and a sign that you feel at home. I can make sure he stays."

"If you can make him stay, sister, we will be eternally grateful! There is nothing finer than being together forever with the one you love."

That evening, the unsuspecting partridge returned. The turtles crowded around to welcome him. The one who thought she was smarter than the others stepped forward.

"Dear Partridge, we missed you so much today, and we are so happy to see you again! It is, quite simply, not as nice on this island without you. You are our best friend. And best friends should always be together, shouldn't they? But as soon as it is light, you leave and you do not return until much later, when we are asleep. We are best friends, but we spend no time together—and that is a terrible thing!"

"I have missed all of you too," replied the partridge, "but I am a bird. I cannot help flying away in search of food. That is why I have wings. Birds rest only at night, when they sleep."

"But, dear Partridge . . . how should I put this? Yes, you are indeed a bird. But what good are your wings to you? You fly back and forth, but it does you very little good. What is truly important for every creature is rest! That is why you landed here with us. And that is why we became friends, so that you too can have the rest you deserve. What if you were attacked and eaten up? Then we would never see you again!"

"But what do you expect me to do about it?" asked the partridge.

"I have the solution: pluck the feathers from your wings! Then you cannot fly away again and you will stay in our company forever. You will no longer have to fly high into the sky. You will be with us, eating with us, drinking with us, waking with us in the morning, and sleeping with us at night. You will truly become one of us."

They are right, thought the partridge. *Why should I make so much effort to go away and come back again when I could just stay here with my friends?*

One by one, he pulled the feathers out of his wings, until the turtle said it was enough. The turtles plucked the feathers he could not reach with his beak. From that day on, the partridge lived among the turtles, enjoying earthly pleasures and the delights of rest.

But then . . . one day a weasel appeared. The weasel peeked out at the partridge from among the branches and thought: *Aha! What do we have here? A plump and juicy bird! And it has already been plucked too!* He rubbed his eyes to make sure he was not dreaming. Then he darted toward the partridge—and seized the bird in his mouth!

The partridge shrieked and screamed: "Help! Help! I am being eaten! Help me, turtles! Help me, my friends!"

The turtles were shocked to see the weasel, and they quickly hid inside their shells.

"Turtles! Help me!" cried the partridge. "Do something!"

"What can we do to protect you from a weasel? Nothing!" was what the turtles shouted back—they did sound sad about it though.

The partridge understood that the turtles could not help him. "You are not to blame, my dear friends. This is my own stupid fault. I deserve this fate because I chose to listen to you. I was the one who pulled out the feathers that might have allowed me to fly away. If I had not done so, the weasel would never, ever have been able to catch me. I do not blame you for anything. Once again, it is not your fault."

Much to his own surprise, with one last burst of energy, the partridge managed to wriggle out of the weasel's mouth and run away. The weasel gazed longingly at the fleeing partridge, and just before the bird disappeared, the weasel shouted after him: "Hey! It's just as well you pulled your feathers out only in a story and not for real. A plucked partridge could never have escaped from my mouth in real life!"

The partridge grew back his feathers lickety-split and flew away only every now and then. But he usually returned to the island in the evening. And that was enough for the turtles. Never again did they suggest that he should change for them. 🐞

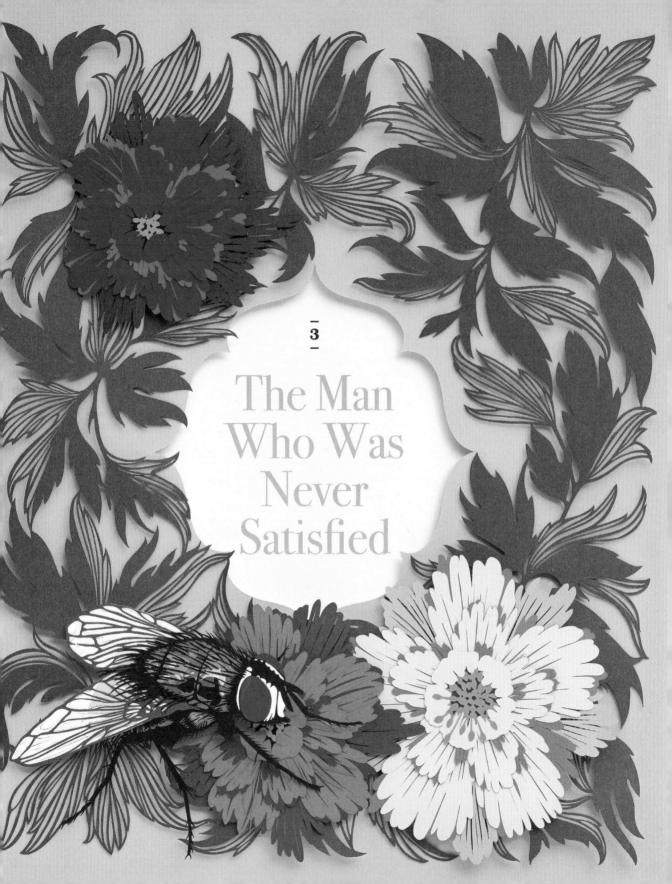

3

The Man
Who Was
Never
Satisfied

One day, long ago, the king of the land suddenly became tired of everyone always bowing whenever he went past and stopping whatever they were doing. He was annoyed that they only said nice things about him, and he wanted to find out what the people of his country were like when there was no king around. He decided it was time for him to get to know his subjects better, and so he put on old clothes and went in search of some ordinary folk.

In the village he chose to visit, there lived a man who had everything anyone could wish for, but still he was never satisfied. He had fine clothes, a big house on the village square with lots and lots of rooms, and a beautiful garden full of flowers, and on the outskirts of the village he also owned a small farm with a vegetable garden, where he grew all kinds of things. But even though he was so rich, he was not satisfied.

On the day the king visited the village, the man who was never satisfied was sitting on a bench in front of his house. He gave the king a smile and a nod. Of course, he did not know it was the king who was walking by.

He just saw a poor stranger in old clothes, and he felt sorry for him. He asked him if he was hungry or thirsty, and when the king said he could do with a bite of food or a drop to drink, he gave him some bread and milk.

The next day, the king returned to the village—this time in his royal robes and with his crown on his head—and he knocked at the man's door. When the man opened up and saw who was standing there, he fell to his knees to show his respect for the king. "Stand up, my good man," the king said to him. "Yesterday I came to your village in my old rags. No one asked me where I was from or how I was doing—no one, except for you. When you heard I was hungry and thirsty, you gave me food and drink. And now I would like to give you something in return. Leave your house and run as far as you can out of the village, and do not stop until you can run no farther. All the land from where we are standing to where you stop will belong to you."

The man could not believe his ears. *I will be the richest man in the village!* he thought happily. *I know I have quite a good life, but after today I will at last be truly satisfied.* "This is the happiest day of my life," he said to the king. "When can I start running?"

"Now!" said the king. "Run—as far as you can!"

The man began to run. He ran along streets and alleyways, past houses and farms, and out of the village. Now and then, he looked back and he thought: *No, it is not far enough yet.*

He ran until he was so far away that he could no longer see his house and the palm trees of his village, and farther still, but every time he looked back, he thought: *No, it's not far enough!*

He ran past date palm trees and fields where goats ate the leaves from the bushes. He ran farther and farther, but still he thought: *Come on! Run farther! This is not far enough!* He was panting, and the muscles in his legs were aching, but still he was not satisfied. He fixed his eyes on the horizon, and all he wanted to do was to run on and on and on. He did not think about his legs or his feet or his lungs, but about the land that would belong to him if he went on running. He ran until he could no longer feel his body. He ran until he lost everything.

The man who could not be satisfied lost all that he had—because he dropped down dead.

"If you are satisfied with what you have, then you are rich."

That was what the people in the village always said to one another. And if anyone claimed it was not true, they told the story of the dissatisfied man who had lived in their village long ago. The story of the man who had once been perfectly healthy and wealthy, but who had dropped down dead because he was never satisfied. 🪲

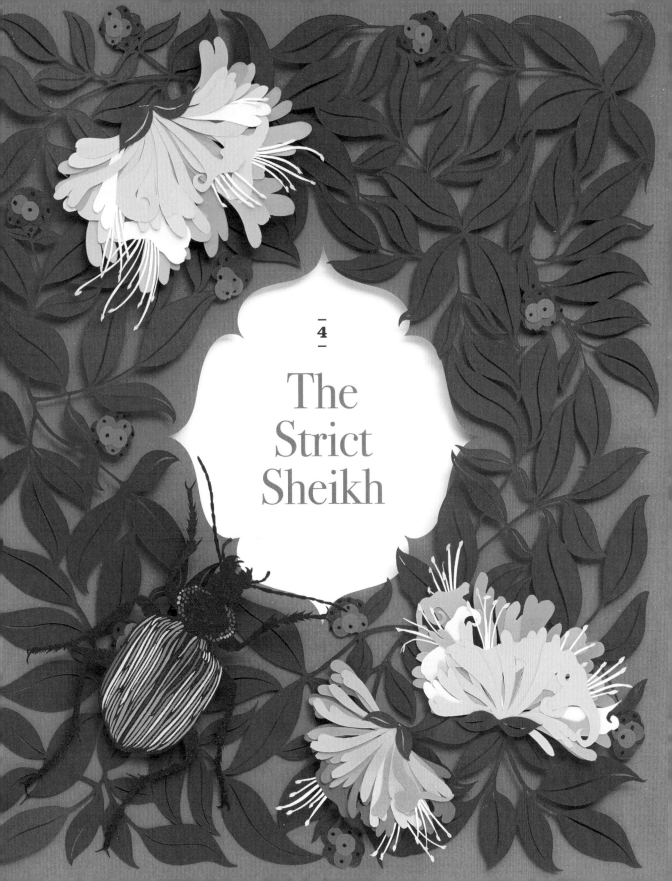

4

The Strict Sheikh

According to Muslims, God created the shrine of Al Kaaba so that all Muslims of every color and every language could walk around it together, their hearts united by one thing: their love for God.

In the endless desert surrounding Al Kaaba, there once lived a Muslim sheikh. He prayed five times a day, read the Koran, and often declared that God was the only one and the greatest one. But instead of loving God, he feared him. Day and night, he repeated to everyone who would listen that those who do exactly as God says will go to heaven and that those who do not will go to hell, where they will burn for a thousand years. The sheikh was very, very strict. And no one, no one at all, could convince him that God is love. And that God does not want anyone to be afraid of him. And that God wants people to love him.

One day the strict sheikh was walking along the road. When he heard a herder praying inside his tent, he stopped to listen.

"My dearest, most beautiful God, I love you more than my sheep and goats. I love you even more than my camels, and more than my beloved donkey too. Oh, dear God, you are my treasure. But where are you? I want so much to take care of you. I want to clean your shoes and make them shine. I want to wash your dirty clothes and hang them on the line to dry. I want to kill all the lice in your hair. And to give you the tastiest milk from my favorite cow. Oh, God, where are you? Tell me, so that I may tidy and clean your house. You are so kind and so good to everyone and everything, and I love you more than my flute and my stick."

That was how the herder prayed, and his prayer came straight from his heart.

As the strict sheikh listened, he became angrier and angrier. His cheeks puffed up with fury, and his eyes nearly popped out of his head. The veins on his forehead grew big and red, and his hands shook more and more. He strode up to the tent and screamed at the herder: "Hey, you! You fool! You idiot!"

Shocked, the herder stumbled out of his tent and looked at the strict sheikh, who by that point had turned completely purple.

"Who do you think you are talking to? So rude! So uncivilized! Do you think that God, who made the heavens and the earth, is unable to take care of himself? Do you think that he, the Almighty, needs you to tidy and clean his house? An ignorant herder who stinks of dung? Do you think that God has shoes that might be dusty? That he has clothes that you could wash? Do you think he has hair with lice in it and that he spends all day scratching his head?"

The strict sheikh whacked the herder on the head with his walking stick, and still he went on yelling: "Never talk like that to God again! Or he not only will be angry with you but will punish the whole world!"

The herder felt the greatest regret of his entire life, and also the greatest fear. He kneeled down. Not to God this time but to the sheikh. He cried and he begged. "Oh, please forgive me for not being polite to God!"

The sheikh hit the herder again. "You fool! Now you are making God even angrier. You are kneeling for my forgiveness, when you should be kneeling for his! Kneel before him! He is the one you should beg for forgiveness!"

Muttering to himself, the strict sheikh walked on, and for a long time, he could hear the herder behind him, still wailing and pleading.

That night, God came to the sheikh in a dream. God was very sad. He stood before the strict sheikh and said, "Do you know why I am so miserable? Because of you, I have lost my finest and purest believer. Because of you, I have lost the herder's heart."

The sheikh awoke in tears. He returned to the herder, kneeled before him, and said: "Please, my dear herder, forgive me, and teach me how to be good to God."

The Three Princes of Serendip

5

Have you heard the story of the three princes of Serendip? They were three very smart princes indeed. Their father, the king, thought it was important for them to know a lot, and he made sure that they were taught by the greatest scholars in the city. You could find no smarter princes for many miles around.

One day, when the princes were old enough and had learned everything that there was to learn from the scholars, their father thought it would be a good idea if his sons were given the opportunity to use their knowledge in real life. He knew they would not simply leave and go out into the world by themselves, so he pretended he had had enough of them and that he wanted to be alone for a while. "Go away!" he growled at the three princes. "And do not return until it is time to return!"

The three princes of Serendip packed their belongings and went out into the big, wide world. As they were so smart, everyone—including their father—thought that they would manage fine wherever they were and that their smartness would open up the world for them. And now you must be wondering: *Well? Was that what happened?*

Well, listen and judge for yourself . . .

The three princes decided to go visit Emperor Beramo in the land of Persia. They hid their crowns and expensive robes in their bags, as they wanted people to kneel before their smartness and not before their crowns. Wearing ordinary clothes, they set off on foot for the capital city of Persia.

They were almost at their destination when, just outside the city, they met a camel driver who had lost his camel. The man was very sad because the animal was all he had.

"Where is my camel?" he wailed, so loudly that everyone could hear. "Who has seen my camel? Dear people, where is my camel?"

"Why don't we play a prank on him?" one of the princes asked his brothers. And the other two thought that sounded like a fine idea.

"Oh, camel driver," said the first prince, "this camel of yours, is it by any chance blind in one eye?"

The camel driver immediately stopped wailing.

Thank goodness! There was some news about his camel. "Yes! That is right," he said. "My camel is indeed blind in one eye!"

The prince smiled. "And does it have a missing tooth?"

"Indeed!" cried the excited camel driver. "My camel is missing a tooth!"

"And does your camel have a limp?"

"Yes, yes, yes! Tell me more! Tell me more!"

"Was it carrying butter on one side and honey on the other?"

"Yes! Indeed!" The man kneeled down gratefully before the three princes. "That is my camel. Now please tell me where it is."

"Your camel?" exclaimed the prince. "How should we know where it is? We have never even seen your camel before."

Well, the camel driver did not understand this at all. "Liars!" he screamed. "Thieves! You have stolen my camel and sold it to someone."

He was furious, and he called in the city guards. The guards surrounded the three princes and took them prisoner.

"What is going on here?" asked Emperor Beramo, who saw the procession of guards marching through the city with their prisoners.

"My lord, I have lost my camel," said the camel driver, who was following the procession. "And these are the thieves who stole it."

"How do you know it was these men who stole your camel?"

"My camel is blind in one eye, has a missing tooth, walks with a limp, and is carrying butter on one side and honey on the other. And these thieves described it perfectly. That cannot be a coincidence!"

"Did you really tell him all those things, about the camel missing a tooth and so on?"

"We did," said the princes.

"So where is the animal?"

"We have no idea. As we have already said, we have never seen the camel."

"I do not believe you," said the emperor. "You are not only thieves but also liars." And, showing no mercy, he had them thrown straight into jail.

Fortunately, the judge also wanted to hear the other side of the story. "If what you claim is true, and you have never seen the camel, then how can you know that it is blind in one eye, has a missing tooth, and walks with a limp?"

"Your Honor, on our journey to your beautiful city we saw that some of the grass on one side of the road had been eaten, while the other side had been left untouched. So we joked that the camel that had passed that way must be blind in one eye."

"And there were lots of tufts of grass left behind that were about the size of a camel's tooth," said the second prince. "So we worked out that the camel must be missing a tooth."

"And the footprints spoke plainly: the camel must have a limp," said the third.

"But how did you know what kind of load the camel was carrying?" asked the judge.

"There were ants all along one side of the road. Butter had clearly been leaking there. And on the other side of the road were drops of honey, with flies swarming around. That was how we knew what the camel was carrying."

The judge was deeply impressed by their smartness. "These men are not the thieves of your camel," he said to the camel driver, "but they will be able to find it for you. You should have listened to them before calling them thieves."

The judge released the three princes, and because they did not bear a grudge, they decided to help the camel driver. They followed the trail left by the camel, and lo and behold, after a while they found it. It was standing in a quiet little valley, grazing away.

The man hugged the three princes and ran to his camel.

And the three princes of Serendip? They smiled and decided it was time to go home. 🪰

6

The Lion
and
the Bull

There was once a little girl called Zahra, who could not sleep if her mother had not told her a story. She loved stories: the better the story was, the more deeply she slept. And her mother could tell better stories than anyone else—short ones and long ones, beautiful ones and exciting ones, mysterious ones and funny ones—and as her warm voice flowed on, she stroked Zahra's black hair. That was perhaps the best thing about story time.

"Mommy, what's the difference between light and darkness?" asked Zahra one evening.

"That's not so hard to answer," her mother replied. "In the light, the heart finds its way through life. In the darkness, the heart finds its way to peace."

"I don't understand, Mommy. Can you tell me a story about it?"

And of course her mother knew a story about it!

"At the end of a long day, a farmer left his bull in the cowshed. It had been a fine day, with plenty of sunshine, but now there were dark clouds hanging over the land. Before long it began to rain. Not just a few drops but buckets and buckets of rain poured down from the sky that night.

"In the valley where the farm was, there also lived a lion. The lion growled angrily when it began to rain. He was annoyed because soon his mane would be dripping with water and that meant he would be cold all night. At that moment he was walking past the cowshed. *Hmm,* he thought, *why don't I just go shelter in there? Not for long, just for a moment, until it stops raining. Then I will stay warm and dry.*

"The lion crept into the shed very quietly, but still the bull noticed him right away. The bull ran outside, into the rain, because he would rather be cold and wet than eaten all up. The lion was glad to see him go. He rested his head on the straw and was soon happily snoring away.

"The farmer was already in bed too but, hearing the heavy rain outside, he decided to dash out and see how his bull was doing.

"He walked into the shed in the darkness and felt around for the animal. He found the head, touched the hairy neck, the strong legs, and the tail, and felt completely reassured: his bull was fine.

"The lion, who had woken up by now, kept silent in the darkness and grinned to himself. *Ah, that poor farmer,* he thought. *He has no idea who or what he is touching. He thinks I am his bull! It is pitch-dark and the darkness gives him peace. But if the light were to shine for a moment, the shock would make him faint.*

"So, Zahra, that is how important light is, and how much peace is to be found in darkness."

Zahra's mother stroked her daughter's black locks once more. "Thank you, Mommy," whispered the girl out of the darkness, already half asleep. "Now I know the difference between light and darkness. Now I can sleep in peace."

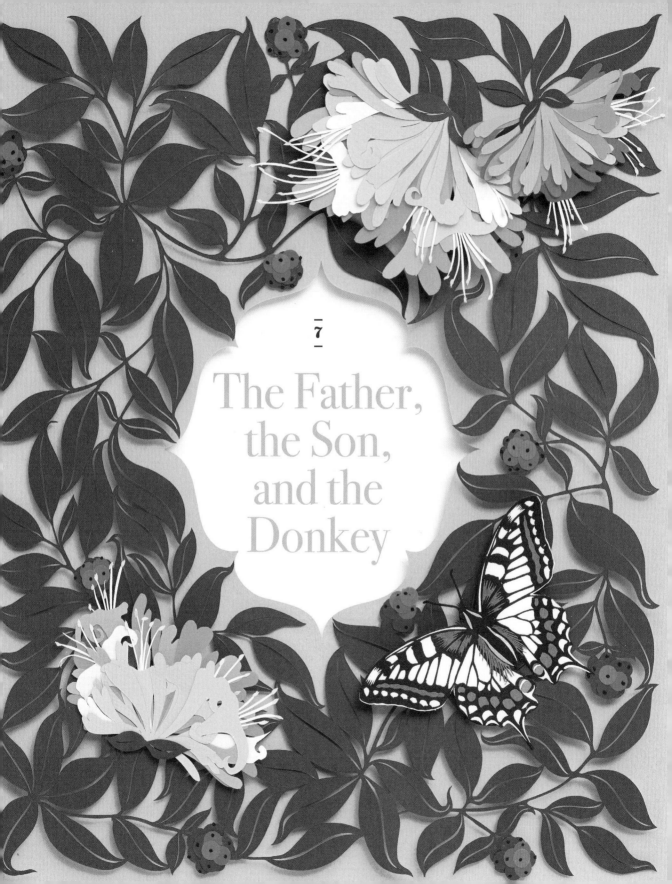

7

The Father, the Son, and the Donkey

Once there was a very beautiful girl named Sousan who lived in a city where the balconies were filled with flowers, the shutters looked like butterflies, and the windows were always open for the fresh breeze to blow through. Sousan thought everything she saw was beautiful. Everyone loved her and she loved everyone, and she helped everyone she could.

One day, she went to visit her grandmother. The boys in the street called after her. "Hey, look at that strange girl over there in that ugly dress!"

Shocked, Sousan fled into her grandmother's house.

"Oh, Sousan, don't pay any attention to them," her grandmother said. "It's not a bad thing if someone doesn't like you! It doesn't matter if someone doesn't think you're beautiful. Not everyone will always love you. And that's not a problem. It's simply how the world works, and if you're at peace with that, it's fine. Just as long as you know yourself that you're a lovely girl with a good heart."

But Sousan did not want to believe her. "But, Grandmother," she said, "I don't understand. I love everyone, so why doesn't everyone love me?"

"Some people think differently than you," her grandmother replied. "Or they look at things differently.

Or they *are* different. So when that happens, don't be disappointed." Sousan shrugged. And her grandmother, who could see that Sousan was not convinced, said, "Wait, I'll tell you a story."

And she began: "Once upon a time, a father and his son were traveling to Baghdad, the city of One Thousand and One Nights. They left their village and went straight across the desert to the other side, the father sitting on the donkey and the son walking beside them. They passed oases and sand dunes and eventually they came to a village.

"In that first village, the people watched them go by and called out, 'What a wicked man! Look! He is making his son walk while he is sitting comfortably on the donkey!'

"The father and the son heard the people talking and did not like what they heard. So before they came to the next village, the father climbed down from the donkey and let his son sit on it while he walked beside it.

"But in that village too, the people watched them go by and had something to say about it: 'What a bad son! Look at him sitting there on the donkey and making his old father walk. If he is not considerate of his father now, when will he ever learn?'

"The father and the son heard the people talking, and before they came to the third village, they both climbed up onto the donkey together.

"But the people in the third village had something to say too. 'What on earth is going on? Look at that poor donkey! That man and that boy are both sitting on him. They're going to break his back! Why won't they think of the poor animal? Can't they take turns sitting on him?'

"The father and the son heard this too. And what do you think they did? Before they came to the next village, they climbed down from the donkey and both walked beside it.

"The people in that village looked at them in surprise and then at one another. Then they burst out laughing!

"'Unbelievable! Just look at that! Don't that man and his son know that donkeys are for riding on, not for walking beside? What a couple of fools!'

"The father and the son heard the people talking, and they had finally learned their lesson.

"'Father,' said the son, 'it does not matter what we do. People always have an opinion about it.'

"The father smiled. 'Exactly, my son, so we must not listen to others, but to our donkey's back and our own hearts. If the donkey's back does not hurt and our hearts do not hurt either, then what we are doing is right.'

"The father and the son smiled, and the donkey brayed. 'And if this is the lesson we have learned, then our journey has been worth it,' said the father. And he turned his face to the sun, which was shining down upon that beautiful day."

Sousan smiled. "That was a lovely story, Grandmother," she said, "but now I'm going back outside to play."

The Poor
Woodcutter

8

There was once, long ago, a woodcutter who was called Abdullah. He lived with his wife and two sons in a forest. Every day he went out with his axe and his donkey. These were the only things he owned. By chopping wood, he made just enough money to feed his wife and children.

I do not want to be a woodcutter all my life, he thought every day. *I do not want to do the same thing forever.*

Sometimes, when he had truly had enough of his life, instead of going to chop wood, he went out in search of good fortune. He would ride his donkey into the valley and shout: "Hey, good fortune! Are you out there? Please come to me!" But the only answer was the echo of his own voice. Sometimes he went up the mountain, stuck his head into the deepest cave, and shouted, "Good fortune! Are you sleeping in here? It is time to wake up!"

But he heard nothing, not even an echo.

Sometimes he rode his donkey to the river and called out, "Good fortune, please flow my way at last!"

But all he heard was the babbling of the water.

Sometimes he traveled to the edge of the desert and shouted to the horizon, "Good fortune! I am here!"

On such days, he returned home without so much as a single twig.

"What have you been doing all day, Abdullah?" his wife, Nazieha, would ask him.

"I was searching for my good fortune," he would say in a disappointed voice.

"Oh, Abdullah, just go to work. Good fortune is of no use to you. It cannot be used to buy anything—and we need food and drink, don't we?"

"But all my hard work isn't helping us either," Abdullah would reply.

So one day, he decided just to stop working.

"I am not doing anything more. There is no point anyway. I am going to stay in bed."

Nazieha tried to persuade him at least to chop down just one tree, but Abdullah turned over and refused to leave his bed.

A man from the next village saw the donkey standing by the house and knocked at the door.

"Hey, Nazieha," he said, "I see that your donkey is standing here. So Abdullah must be at home."

"That's right. He does not want to work today," said Nazieha with a sigh. "He is tired from chasing after good fortune."

"Then may I borrow your donkey for the day?"

"Yes, of course. Take him with you."

So the man took the donkey and snuck off to a deserted field where he knew a treasure lay buried beneath a lonely date palm tree. He began digging there and dug away until he hit a sack with hundreds of gold 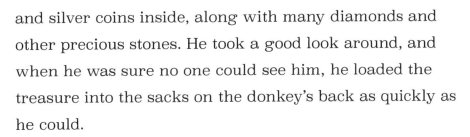 and silver coins inside, along with many diamonds and other precious stones. He took a good look around, and when he was sure no one could see him, he loaded the treasure into the sacks on the donkey's back as quickly as he could.

He walked the donkey back to the village, and as he was thinking about everything he could buy with the treasure, he spotted the king's banner in the distance. Two soldiers came toward him. He knew that the treasure he had dug up actually belonged to the king and that he would be condemned to death if he were caught with all that gold, so he ran away, leaving the donkey behind.

The donkey had no idea what was happening and calmly plodded on. He plodded and plodded until the sun set and he was standing at the door of his house.

Nazieha looked out the window and saw the donkey with his heavy load. She went outside and opened one of the sacks. Her breath caught in her throat when she saw the gold and the diamonds glinting up at her.

"Abdullah! A treasure! Your fortune is here!" she called.

"Fortune? Never mention that word in this house again!" Abdullah shouted angrily from his bed.

"But good fortune has come to us, Abdullah!" cried Nazieha. "Come take a look!"

Abdullah climbed out of bed and could not believe his eyes. There was so much gold and silver and so many glittering stones that he would never have to work another day in his life. He could live like a king.

"You see!" he said to Nazieha. "If you chase after good fortune, it runs away from you, but turn your back on good fortune, and it will come to you."

9

The Lost Necklace

Two friends, Nabil and Samer, were traveling through the desert. The night was clear and the moon was gleaming. They told each other stories to stay awake so that they did not fall from their animals and tumble to the ground.

"Have you heard the story of the lost necklace?" Nabil, sitting on his camel, asked Samer, who was riding on a donkey beside him.

"No," said Samer. "Please tell it to me!"

"In the land of the Nile," Nabil began, "there once lived a queen, who had a lady-in-waiting called Soureya. Soureya was smart, beautiful, and kind, so she had succeeded in making her way up through the ranks in the palace. From a position as a poor serving girl, who spent her days in the laundry room in the basement, she had moved closer and closer to the queen, eventually becoming her companion. Soureya helped the queen with everything. At first, she was proud of herself and happy to have made it so far, but it was not long before she found herself wishing she had never even come to live at the palace. This is what happened.

"One day, the queen wanted to take a bath. She got undressed, dropped her clothes onto the floor, and laid her gold necklace on top of them. 'Take good care of my necklace,' she said to Soureya, who hurried to pick up the queen's things. 'It is my most precious possession. I received it from my mother, and she from her mother, and she from her mother, all the way back through seven mothers.'

"While the queen was in the bath, Soureya neatly folded the queen's clothes in the bedroom next door, and she kept a close eye on the necklace as she did so. Now and then, she picked it up and let the beautiful golden beads gleam in the sunshine. The queen took her time. In fact, she took so long that Soureya became thirsty. She decided to fetch some water and slipped the necklace under the prayer mat for safety. Soureya was away for just a minute, no longer than that, but it was enough. For she had not noticed that a magpie, attracted by the glint of the golden beads, had come closer. And one minute was all the magpie needed.

"He pulled the necklace out from under the prayer mat with his beak and flew with it to the window ledge, where he played with it for a while, before hiding it inside a crack in the wall.

"Meanwhile, the queen had spent so long in the bath that her fingers had become as wrinkled as an old woman's. She called Soureya to come dry her and dress her, but much to Soureya's horror, when she went to take the gold necklace from under the prayer mat, it was no longer there.

"The queen screamed and screamed when she realized her treasured gold necklace was gone. 'Soureya! You thief! You have stolen my necklace! And after I had told you it was my most precious possession!'

"'No, my queen, I did not! Truly I did not!' sobbed Soureya. 'I did not take the necklace. I hid it under the mat so it would not be lost.'

"But the queen refused to listen. 'I trusted you,' she shrieked, 'but I should never have done so. You are an untrustworthy snake. No punishment is severe enough for you. I will have you thrown into jail for the rest of your life!'

"And so Soureya ended up in a cell, because no matter how many times she said she had not stolen anything, the queen did not believe her. Neither did the king, because the more powerful and wealthy people are, the less they listen to others and the more important they think themselves.

"No one can say how long Soureya was in jail. She cried and was miserable inside that gloomy cell with its thick walls and just one tiny window with bars that occasionally let in a little sunlight and warmth. She regretted that she had ever wanted to be close to the queen. It had brought her power and prosperity for a time, but now she was more wretched than ever before.

"Years passed and Soureya remained in her cell, with nothing to eat and drink but bread and water, and she was sure she would never be free again.

"But do you know what the strange thing is? Even though the truth sometimes disappears from sight, in the end it will reveal itself once more. And that is what happened in this case.

"One morning, when the king and queen were still in their bedroom, they heard tapping and rustling at the window. They walked over there and saw a magpie pulling

something out of a crack in
the wall—the sparkling gold necklace
that had passed from mother to daughter
until it came to the queen. The magpie
was so startled to see the two faces at the
 window that it dropped the necklace.
All the queen had to do was pick it up, and
she had her precious heirloom once more.

"'Poor Soureya!' the queen exclaimed. 'So she
was telling the truth! All that time in jail, and she was
innocent! We must release her at once.'

"The queen felt so awful about having let her
companion waste away in a dark cell for years and years
that she invited Soureya to live in the palace with her and
the king as their daughter. But Soureya did not care for
that idea at all—and she made sure the queen knew that!

"'But then what do you want? Just tell me. I will give
you whatever you wish for,' said the queen, who was
feeling very guilty indeed.

"'My queen, I know exactly what I want. In jail I
learned that I do not belong in this palace. I belong in my
village, far from here. I just want to go home.'

"And the doors of the palace opened up for her. Full of relief, Soureya headed outside, happy to leave behind all the power and wealth. Now her life could really begin!

"So be on your guard, Samer, if you ever find yourself in the company of the rich and powerful, because life can suddenly take a nasty turn.

"Samer? Are you still awake?"

Nabil glanced around. Only the donkey was walking beside him. When he looked back, he saw Samer lying on the ground some distance behind, dozing in the light of the full moon.

He must have missed at least half of the story! Nabil turned his camel and rode back. Then he climbed down, lay on the ground beside Samer, and went to sleep as well.

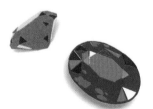

10

The
Beautiful
City

Once upon a time, there was a magnificent city. It was the most beautiful city in the world. The city lay between two rivers. In the winter there were songs, in the summer there was fruit, in the spring there were rainbows, and in the fall there were colors. God often looked down from heaven at that city and thought: *Ah, a paradise on earth. How wonderful.*

However, out in the desert, there lived a sheikh called Noureddine. He believed that paradise could exist only high in the heavens, near God, and not on earth among ordinary mortals. And he also believed that you could only get into heaven after plenty of pain, poverty, and misery, not after a lifetime filled with happiness.

He heard of the fine city and thought: *It is too bad that the people who live there do not know that their life in that beautiful city will lead them to hell. I must warn them and show them the way to heaven.*

So Sheikh Noureddine climbed onto his camel and rode toward the beautiful city. He rode for weeks and weeks and months and months, and when he finally arrived, he saw that it was indeed the most beautiful city in the world.

There was water rippling and babbling all around. The women were all happy, swimming in the river, splashing one another, and laughing. The men were all full of joy, making music and singing. The children ran and played. The birds colored the branches with their fine feathers and the heavens with their songs.

The sheikh looked at his reflection in the water of a lake. He was dusty, he had wild eyebrows and a shaggy beard, and his clothes were old and torn. Then he looked at the beautiful people having fun and thought, *It really is too bad that their happiness will send all these people to hell, where they will burn for all eternity.*

"Come over here, my good man. Eat with us and listen to the music," a man called to him.

"Hey there, friend, come into the water and wash that dust off you," a woman shouted from the water.

Trembling, the sheikh fell to his knees and prayed to God. "Oh, God, they are trying to lead me astray with their sinful life, but they will not succeed."

He thanked the people for their offers, but said that such behavior was not right for him.

"So what is right for you?"

"Eternal happiness in heaven after death. This happiness here, in this life, is false and wicked."

"Oh, don't be such a spoilsport," shouted a woman. "God created all this beauty so we could enjoy it, didn't he?"

Sheikh Noureddine shook his head. "Such ignorance," he whispered, full of pity. "I must take the time to convince them."

Just outside the city he found a cave, where he went to live. Every day he returned to the city, and whenever he met someone, he would strike up a conversation with them. He told them that you could only get into heaven after much misery and sorrow, and that beauty and happiness do not lead to God. Slowly, one by one, he began to convince the people of the city.

Years passed and, because of the sheikh, the beautiful, happy city changed into a gray and gloomy place. There were no women swimming or laughing. There were no men making music or singing songs. No one leaned out a window with a happy smile on their face, and no one celebrated, not even when a child was born, because—or so they believed—the baby had been born into a world that was meant to be miserable and poor and sad. People began to hide away in cellars and barns and caves to pray and to ask God for mercy.

This city has found its way to God, thought the sheikh, *and now I can leave with an easy heart.* He climbed onto his camel and headed off to the desert.

After some time, he saw a man standing at the side of the road. He was dressed in white clothes, and he looked gray and sad.

Who is that man? the sheikh wondered. *I do not recognize him. I shall stop and talk to him. Maybe I can show him the way to God.*

The sheikh climbed down from his camel and walked toward the man. "Who are you?" he asked.

"Do you not recognize me?" replied the man.

"No, I do not. But I can see that you look sad and have tears in your eyes."

"I am God," said the man. "And look behind you. You have transformed a glorious city into a dark and gloomy ruin. And why? To show people the way to me? And yet now you stand before me and do not even recognize me! So how can you show others the way?"

The sheikh looked at God—and now he saw the light that was shining from him. He kneeled down. "Oh, God, forgive me," he said.

"I do," God replied. "But remember that it is happiness and love that lead to me, and not your dark thoughts."

"Oh, God, forgive me," Sheikh Noureddine whispered again, and he whispered it and whispered it and went on whispering it, and he is still whispering it even now.

11

Sindibad

L ong ago, in Baghdad, where the streets, alleyways, and markets are filled with the colors and smells of herbs and spices and where you can find beautiful fabrics, jewels, and fruits from distant lands, there lived a boy called Sindibad.

Sindibad did not like to go to school. Not because he did not wish to learn, as he was actually very smart, but because he preferred to roam the streets.

"Go to school and study a profession," his father and mother said to him.

"I do not need to study anything," he would always reply. "I can pick up everything I need as I go along." And then he headed off on another walk through the streets and the markets of Baghdad.

One day he heard some market traders talking about a hidden treasure—jewels, gold coins, and diamonds. No one knew where this treasure was concealed, but as the traders said, "Seek and you will find."

Sindibad decided that he had seen enough of Baghdad and that it was time to set off into the big, wide world, in search of the treasure he had heard the traders talking about.

His mother, his father, and his brother and sisters said farewell to him with heavy hearts. He was still young, and they did not know when he would return home or if they would ever see him again.

"I will come back," he reassured them, carrying the knapsack his mother had filled on his shoulder. "I am certain of that. But I will not be the boy I am now. I will be different—richer and older and wiser!"

"Promise me you will do one thing before you leave Baghdad!" his father called after him.

Sindibad, who always listened to his father, stopped in the gateway. "What do you want me to do?"

"I have sent for the wise man. Wait here for him and listen to his advice!"

"I will, Father!" said Sindibad, and before he set off on his journey, he did indeed listen to the wise man's advice.

The wise man could look into people's hearts and minds and read their thoughts and feelings.

"Oh, Sindibad," said the wise man, "you have just said farewell to your home and your family. Do you not know that what you are seeking is always closer than you think?"

"I am sure you are right, oh wise one, but still I am going on my journey."

"And what do you expect from this journey?"

"I have heard about a treasure of gold and diamonds, and I am going in search of it."

The wise man smiled. "Sindibad, that treasure too is closer than you think. Seek and you will find, but what you are looking for is more often than not right under your feet!"

Sindibad looked down at his sandals and laughed.

"Thank you for the advice, wise man. I shall keep it in mind!"

Sindibad walked to the banks of the Tigris and boarded a ship, which took him to the Gulf. There he went aboard a larger ship, which carried him to the ocean. And from that ocean he traveled to other oceans in every shade of blue. He went

from island to island and from harbor to harbor. Then he traveled from mountain to mountain and from desert to desert. He grew older and older, but he never gave up his search for the treasure. Every time he thought he was close, people said, "There's still a way to go." Then he would travel on, and people would say, "Just a little farther."

One day he saw a caravan. "Where are you headed? Where are you from? And what is your name?" the camel drivers asked.

"My name is Sindibad, I come from Baghdad, and I am searching for a treasure," he replied.

"Ah," said one of the camel drivers. "I once heard a story from a traveler about a man called Sindibad who said farewell to his family and left Baghdad to go looking for a treasure. And just before he set off, his father called him back and told him to listen to a wise man's advice. The wise man told him that the treasure was beneath his feet. The traveler also said that this Sindibad did not listen to the wise man. He should have dug there, exactly where he was standing. If he had done that and had dug a hole exactly twice his own height, then he would have found the treasure."

As the man knew so many things that were true, Sindibad believed his words. He traveled with the caravan back through the desert to Baghdad, until he came to the gateway to his parents' home.

In the exact same spot where he had stood before leaving, he dug a hole twice his own height—and he found the treasure. So it had indeed been right under his feet. All that time, good fortune had been closer than he thought.

—
12
—

Soup

In the middle of the desert, there was once a very small kingdom. It was no more than an oasis. One spring was enough to provide water for the whole kingdom. One donkey was enough to travel through the whole realm. One person's voice was enough to make a story heard from one side of the kingdom to the other. In that small kingdom no one was ever far from anyone else.

Long ago, a king and a queen lived in that realm, which was not only very small but also very beautiful. They had four sons and a daughter. The king always proudly told his children that he would not wish to live anywhere but their own small kingdom. The princes and the princess loved it too, but they were also curious about the world beyond the desert.

"We want to see more of the world, to meet other people, to learn the lessons that life teaches," they said.

"You do not need to travel in order to learn," said the king. "I shall teach you the most important lesson of all. I shall show you what real love is—and then you will know enough."

He told his cooks to make the tastiest soup they could. He made his carpenter build a long table, and the smith was ordered to make forty spoons, each of them three feet long. Then he invited forty people to a royal feast. They were all people who liked to talk about love. But they did not carry love inside their hearts.

That evening, the king, the queen, the four princes, and the princess sat at the table with their forty guests, who all came from the kingdoms beyond the desert. In front of each of them was a bowl of the most delicious soup and, beside it, a spoon that was three feet long. The hungry guests wanted to start the meal, but no one could get even a drop of soup into their mouths with those long spoons. They made a dreadful mess, and at the end of the evening, all forty of them went home with empty stomachs.

When the guests had left, the king's children looked at him with puzzled expressions on their faces. "Just wait," said the king. "Tomorrow we will have a second feast. I have invited forty other guests from the kingdoms beyond the desert. But these ones carry love not only on their lips but also inside their hearts."

The next evening the royal family sat at the long table with the forty visitors who all had love inside their hearts. They were served bowls of the delicious soup too, with exactly the same long spoons. But these people, because of the love inside their hearts, thought not only of themselves and their own hunger but also of others, so they used the long spoons to take some soup from the bowl of the person opposite them, and then they fed it to that person. The person opposite then returned the favor, and so everyone was able to enjoy the delicious soup. And all the guests left the little kingdom with full stomachs.

The king felt satisfied as he sat in his oasis that evening. "Did you see what happened?" he asked his children. "You do not need to learn more than this: if love is in your heart, then soup will fill your stomach."

13

Murat and His Best Friend

In a small village deep in the forest, where the branches form a roof and the leaves embrace, beyond high waterfalls and even farther beyond, that is where Murat lived. His grandfather, who always gave him wise advice, had said that in a village far from the bustling city, it was important to have good friends—friends who would support you when it was needed and who would help you when danger threatened. So Murat asked a boy called Belsem if he would be his best friend.

"That's fine by me," said Belsem.

"Shall we promise each other that we'll always be best friends and never abandon each other?" said Murat.

"Fine by me," said Belsem again.

Murat was happy, because now he had a best friend—a friend who would be sure to help him when needed. Or at least that was what he thought, until he discovered that making real friends is not that easy.

One morning Murat asked Belsem if he would like to go to the waterfalls with him. It was a nice trip, but not without danger, as they had to travel quite a way through the forest.

"Fine by me," said Belsem.

"But if there's a threat of danger, you can't leave me behind," said Murat, "because I'm no good at running away or climbing trees to escape."

"Of course, I wouldn't abandon you," said Belsem.

The two friends took a knapsack filled with bread, hard-boiled eggs, cucumber, and grapes, and they headed off into the forest.

They walked a long way until they came to a lake with water so clear that you could see the fish swimming in it.

Just as Murat was about to shed his clothes and take a dip, a terrifying sound came from the trees behind them. They turned around—and a big bear emerged from among the bushes. Belsem did not pause for a moment but ran straight for a tall tree.

"Belsem! Don't leave me!" called Murat. "We promised each other!"

But Belsem did not listen. He climbed straight up into the tree, as fast as he could.

Murat had little time to think, but he suddenly remembered that his grandfather had once told him that bears do not bite dead bodies. So he fell to the ground and pretended to be dead.

Belsem watched from the tall tree as the big bear walked toward Murat. The bear sniffed at his clothes and his face. Murat held his breath and did not move. He was well aware that this was his only chance. And, soon enough, the bear turned around and disappeared back into the undergrowth.

Not long after that, when the coast
seemed clear, Belsem climbed back
down and walked toward Murat.

"Hey, Murat," he said. "You must have been so scared! It
looked like you fainted and then the bear came and
whispered something to you. What did it say?"

Murat, finally daring to breathe again, stood up and
brushed the sand from his clothes.

"You want to know what the bear said? He said that
real friends don't abandon you," Murat told Belsem, and
then he picked up his knapsack and walked back to the
village.

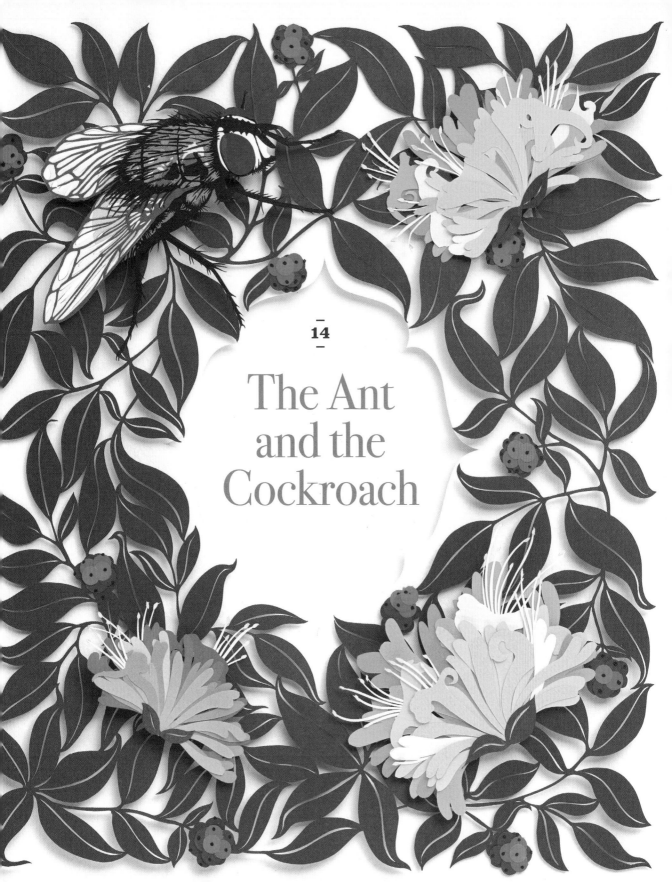

14

The Ant
and the
Cockroach

In a country called Lebanon, where there are beaches and mountains, a little ant once lived in a forest of cedar trees. The ant loved to work. There was nothing she would rather do. She could not sit still but had to keep busy.

"My work is my life," she said. "When I'm working, I feel useful to myself and to others." And she also said, "When I'm working, I know why I'm alive. I can feel, sense, and see the purpose of my life!"

She worked all the spring and all throughout the long summer days, from the moment when the sun rose until it sleepily set. She lugged vine leaves, made piles of sand, built walls, dragged pieces of wood back and forth, fetched food, dug rivers, and walked up and down, looking for work and more work.

Her next-door neighbor was a cockroach. He did not like work at all. All he liked was music—and most of all singing. He sang his songs about the Lebanese valleys and the gentle breeze of the Mediterranean, practiced scales, tuned strings, and played melodies on his violin from the moment he awoke to the moment he fell asleep, which was long after the sun had set.

"Tell me, neighbor Cockroach, do you actually get anything for your music?" the ant asked one day. "I mean, do you make anything for it?"

"Of course I do," the cockroach proudly replied. "I make myself happy. Very, very happy!"

"But do you make any money? Can you earn anything to eat with it? Or to drink? Or a place to sleep? You can't fry up happiness and eat it, can you? I don't believe you can make tea with it either. And as far as I know you can't throw happiness onto the fire and burn it in the chilly wintertime."

The cockroach just laughed.

"Oh, my dear neighbor Ant, how funny you are, even though you always have such a terribly serious look on your face. Do you know what you should do? You should have a bit more fun! Stop working day and night. Work is stupid and dull. Listen to music, sing, or learn to play an instrument! We're born to enjoy ourselves, not to work."

"Oh, I enjoy music, and I like to sing as well, but some of us have to work, you know."

"We don't have to do anything, neighbor Ant. Nothing at all!" said the cockroach.

The beautiful spring days melted away like snow in the sunshine. And though the days of summer lasted long, they were over soon enough. And all that time, the cockroach sang and played his violin while the ant was busily working away.

Then the wet autumn began. The cockroach was just about able to keep himself alive with scraps left by the other animals. But then the harsh winter began, covering the mountains of Lebanon with snow.

It was too cold for the cockroach to go outside. Starving, he walked around in circles inside his house, but there was nothing to eat. He shivered and crawled under his blankets, because he had nothing to put on the fire. He looked in every corner, but all he could find was his violin and the songs he had written, and they would not make his fire burn. Eventually, he struggled through the bleak wind and the freezing cold to the ant's house and knocked at her door.

"Neighbor Ant, please open the door! This cold is killing me!"

The ant opened up and let in the shivering cockroach. Inside her house, the fire was burning away.

The cockroach scuttled over to lie in front of it and warm himself up. "Neighbor Ant, I'm starving to death. Do you have anything I could eat?"

"Of course," said the ant, and she gave him a piece of bread with raisins and honey. "But when spring comes again, don't forget that hard work will get you through the bad days. And during the long days of summer, think about this harsh time of the year every now and then. Because I'm warning you—next winter you won't get anything from me!"

That winter the cockroach visited the ant every night for warmth and a bite to eat. She gave him food, he played the most beautiful tunes for her, and together they sang the most wonderful songs. That was how they spent the winter until spring came around again.

"Could you come here to play your music again next winter?" asked the ant. "Because of your music, I hardly noticed it was winter."

15

The Arrogant Rooster

A very, very, very long time ago and a very, very, very long way from here, there was a large village in the middle of the desert. Can you imagine it? A village on the banks of a lake, in an oasis full of fruit trees and date palms, where the people live in houses of clay and the sound of songbirds can be heard all around—even in the middle of a dry desert!

In that village, there lived a rooster—an arrogant rooster who thought himself terribly important. As darkness slipped away and daylight came, he would jump proudly onto the wall and think: *Now I'm going to wake up everyone and everything!* And he would crow "Cock-a-doodle-doo" as he looked around and thought: *What an amazing creature I am! Without me, everyone and everything would stay asleep.*

Every day, the rooster jumped up onto the wall and crowed until everyone woke up. Every day, he preened his colorful feathers and strutted among his hens with his beak stuck up in the air. Every day, he ate all the fruit that fell from the trees and the bread that people gave him. Until, early one morning, tired of the rooster's noise and arrogance, the farmer grabbed him, stuffed him into a cage, and tied it onto the donkey's back to go sell the rooster in the city.

The rooster stared in horror through the bars of the cage at the village becoming smaller and smaller. *What now?* he thought. *Who's going to wake everyone up?*

All day long, they crossed the desert, and by the time they arrived in the city, it was evening. The next day, they were at the market bright and early, and the farmer tried to sell his rooster. But what do you think happened? No one was interested!

Why does no one want to buy me? the rooster thought, still arrogant at first. *Don't they know that without me no one wakes up? That I even wake the dawn?* But as the day grew longer, he became sadder and sadder. He thought back to his village. To the trees, the blue sky, the clay walls he loved to jump up onto. To his hens and the cool shade of the date palms. And the tasty fruit that fell from the trees. Here in the city it was filthy and noisy. He was sitting in a cage, waiting to be sold. And what would happen then? Would he be eaten? Or kept inside a dirty chicken coop? Could a rooster even crow in the city or would the neighbors start complaining because they wanted to sleep, even though the sun had risen long ago? He grew more and more miserable.

When the day was over, the rooster had still not been sold. The farmer slept one more night in the city and then set off for the village with the caged rooster on the donkey.

At the end of the afternoon, they saw the village and the oasis growing bigger in the distance. As they approached, the rooster felt happier and happier, but when they arrived at the village, he was amazed to see that the whole village was awake! The adults, the children, the goats, the donkeys, the birds in the trees, and all his hens. Everyone was awake! *How can that be?* he thought. *How did they wake up without me?*

When they reached their home, the farmer let the

rooster out of the cage. His hens flocked happily around him, because even though he was arrogant, they still loved him.

"Hey, hens," crowed the rooster, "how did the dawn arrive this morning without any help from me?"

"Oh, just the same as every day," cackled one of the hens. "With you, without you, it doesn't make any difference to the dawn."

"And by the way," said another hen, "you're not the only rooster in the village."

Shocked, the rooster went to sleep, and he was still not quite back to his old self when he woke up the next morning. He decided to pay more attention this time. He jumped up onto the wall, but instead of immediately opening his beak, he listened. In the distance, he heard the other roosters crowing, one by one. *I've been so foolish,* thought the rooster. *I'm not the only one. I was so wrapped up in myself that I didn't even hear all the other roosters. Just listen to that chorus of cock-a-doodle-doos. It's so beautiful!*

He took a deep breath and crowed at the top of his voice. Not to wake everyone up, but just to let the other roosters know that he had heard them.

16

The Man Who Was Thirsty

"We human beings think we're the smartest creatures on earth. Smarter than the animals and smarter than everything around us. That may be true. But no matter how smart we think we are, we're still a bit foolish at times. Sometimes we don't see the solution that's right in front of us," my father said to me one day as we were driving to the city.

I was looking out the window at the cars racing by and at the dry landscape, with the occasional shrub and groups of nomads with their tents and goats. "Remember this when you have a problem," he continued. "Do not stand in the middle of your problem. Just for a moment, stop trying to figure it out. Look around you and then step outside your problem. As soon as you are no longer in the middle of it, you can look at it from a distance. And then the problem is also often the solution. Did I ever tell you the story about the man who was thirsty?"

"No," I said to my father. "Never heard of it."

"Once upon a time," my father began, "on the banks of the Barada, one of the most beautiful rivers in this part of the world, and one that so many poets have written about, there was a high wall. The wall was higher than everything around it, and on top of that wall stood a man. And the man was thirsty.

"The man looked down at the trees on the riverbank, at the grass, the birds, and the animals. *Oh,* he thought, *every living creature can enjoy the river's water. Everything and everyone, except for me. Up here, on this high wall, I can't reach that pure water.*

"Every day the man broke a stone from the wall and threw it into the river. Then he heard the sound of the water below, and he felt better. *And,* he thought, *this means that the wall is a little less high every day.*

"But one day the river had had enough. 'Why do you keep throwing stones into me? You're hurting me!' it cried.

"'Oh, beautiful Barada River,' replied the man who was thirsty, 'I'm throwing stones at you for two reasons: the sound of your wonderful water eases my thirst, and every stone I break from the wall brings me closer to you.'

"'Please, Man,' said the river, 'that's not a solution, is it? Stop and think about it. Instead of demolishing the wall and throwing stones at me, you could climb down here and come drink my water.'

"'Oh!' exclaimed the man who was thirsty. 'Who knew it could be that simple? My goodness, why didn't I think of that?'"

My father laughed. "And now we're going to have something to drink too. Let's stop over there for a glass of tea."

17

Death
and the
Servant

Once upon a time, in Serendip, the most beautiful city in the land, at least according to all the people who lived there and all the travelers who passed through, there was a wealthy and powerful man. This man had a servant who was very dear to him. He treated him not as a servant but as his right-hand man or even his best friend. This servant left the mansion one day to go to the market to buy fruit for his master. On his way there, he whistled happily, for he was healthy and strong and young. And life was still at his feet, not upon his shoulders.

At the busy market, however, he had a huge fright when Death suddenly appeared before him. The servant recognized him at once. Death looked at the servant in surprise, but before he could say a word, the servant dropped everything he was holding and ran back to his master's palace. Shaking with fear, he opened the gate, ran to his mighty lord, and kneeled before him.

"What is wrong?" asked his master.

"Oh, my lord, I went to buy fruit at the market—and I saw Death there."

"And did he say anything to you?" the master said.

"No, not a word. He just looked at me in surprise!"

The master thought this all sounded very risky. "Go quickly to the stables," he said, "and take the strongest and fastest horse, and flee far away, far from Death. Ride as quickly as you can to Baghdad."

So the servant went to the stables, took the strongest and fastest horse, and fled for Baghdad. He rode day and night. He left on Tuesday, made the horse run onward on Wednesday after a short night's rest, spent the following night in the desert, and on Thursday saw the palaces of Baghdad appear on the distant horizon.

He gave a sigh of relief. *Thank goodness,* he thought, *I'll reach Baghdad before Friday!*

That same Thursday, the wealthy man was walking through the market, and there he saw the figure of Death in the same spot where his servant had seen him before.

"Hey, Death!"

"Greetings, wealthy man!"

"You gave my beloved servant quite a fright."

"I did not intend to. I just looked at him in surprise. That was all."

"But why?"

"Because I thought: *What on earth is that man doing here in Serendip? I'm supposed to be meeting him in Baghdad on Friday morning and taking him home with me!*"

The Magic Jugs

18

Remember what I am about to tell you forever and even longer. Remember that nothing is all bad! And if something goes wrong, in the end it can still be for the best. Do not ever forget this! Tell it to whoever will listen to you, and be sure to keep on telling it to yourself as well.

In a small village called Semma, there lived a woman called Noura. She had the most beautiful garden you have ever seen. Fruit trees grew on her piece of land, and she had planted carrots and tomatoes. She grew peppers, eggplants, and beans too, and she never had to go to the market to buy food, since there were enough vegetables growing there to feed both her and her neighbors.

Every day she walked to the well, carrying her two jugs on a yoke. She fetched water for herself and for the plants in her vegetable garden. But what Noura did not know was that her jugs were magical. They were, in fact, the only jugs in the world that could talk, although they rarely did so.

Noura filled the jugs at the well, hung them back on either side of the yoke, and walked home with them.

One of the jugs was perfect. That one was always full of water when Noura got back to the vegetable garden.

However, the other jug was cracked. Water dripped out through the crack, and by the time Noura got home, the jug was only half full. And sometimes, if she had been walking slowly, it was only a  quarter full! This made the jug very sad.

Every day the jug became sadder and sadder, and after some time he could not bear his sadness any longer. When they arrived at the well, he began to cry, and he blurted out to Noura: "I am so, so sorry!"

Noura looked at the jug in surprise. "Whatever is the matter?" she asked.

"I am such a useless jug," sobbed the jug. "You fill me to the brim every day, but while you're walking home, the water leaks out, and so I'm only half full when you get to the place where you need water."

Noura laughed. "Oh, Jug," she said, "instead of being sad, just take a look around you on the way back!"

Noura hung the two jugs on her yoke and set off for home.

The cracked jug looked around
and noticed that there were
flowers blooming all along his
side of the road, but there
were none on the other
jug's side of the road.

"Did you see?" Noura
asked when they got
home. "I saw long ago that
you had a crack. So I sowed
flower seeds by the road, and
thanks to the water that
dripped out through the
crack in your side, I can
always pick beautiful
flowers."

The jug that was perfect and arrived home full of water every day had always been so proud. She had thought herself better than the jug with the crack. But now that she saw what the broken jug had created, she felt jealous, and she too began to cry. Her side of the road was so dusty and dry and nothing ever grew there.

"Oh, Jug," Noura said to her, "are you feeling sorry for yourself now too? It's true. There are no flowers growing on your side of the road, but thanks to you I have the tastiest vegetables in the village growing in my garden!"

"Noura's right," the jugs said to each other. "We both do something good, each in our own way!"

After that day, the jugs never spoke another word. But even without words, they were still magic jugs: one that brought all that water to the vegetable garden, and the other that watered the flowers on the roadside.

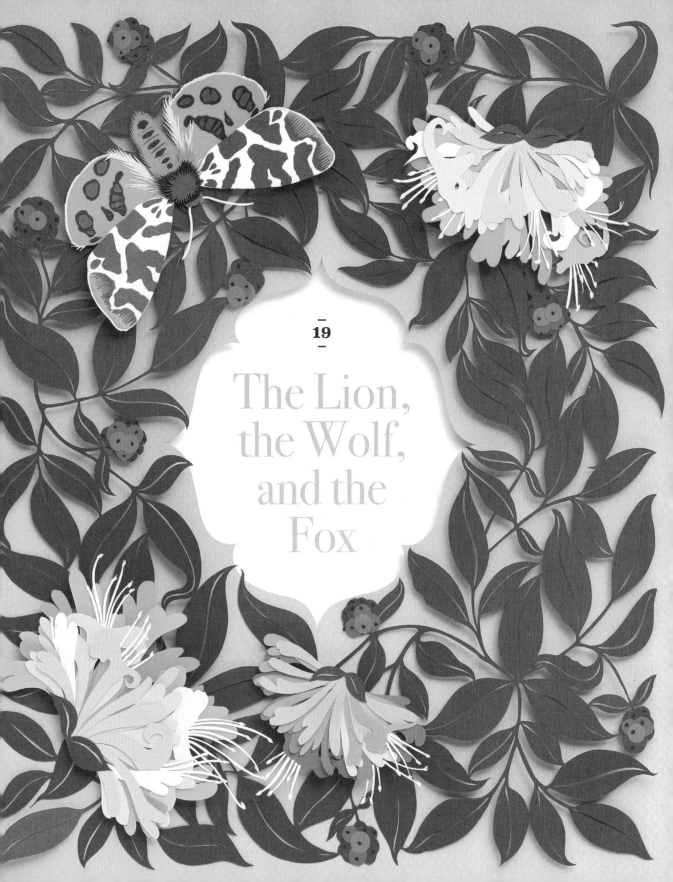

19

The Lion, the Wolf, and the Fox

A lion, a wolf, and a fox decided to go hunting together. They caught a bull, a deer, and a rabbit. Then they lay down under a tree to divide up their catch.

The lion told the wolf to decide who should have what. The wolf smiled and licked his lips. "Lion, you can take the bull. Then I will have the deer, and the fox may have the rabbit."

Furious, the lion rose to his feet. With sparks flying from his eyes, he stalked toward the wolf.

"What are you saying? That is so unfair, Wolf! Where did you learn such behavior? Leave! Now! If you do not disappear this instant, I'll bite through your neck, and you'll never draw breath again!"

The wolf shivered with fear. "I'm so sorry, Mr. Lion. It was a mistake. Forgive me, I'll divide up our catch again!"

"You will do no such thing! Just go!" growled the lion—and then he roared.

The wolf ran until he disappeared over the horizon.

The lion turned around and prowled over to the fox, who had been watching closely.

"Now it's your turn, Fox. Divide the food between the two of us, but fairly, not like that stupid wolf."

"Mr. Lion, Your Majesty," said the fox, bowing down between his front paws, "I'm so delighted that you've given me the honor of dividing our catch."

"Get up," roared the lion, "and share out the goods!"

The fox stood up, feeling both shy and afraid. "Mr. Lion, the bull is for your breakfast, because you need energy for the whole day and have to start the day with a full stomach. The deer is for your lunch, because the deer is smaller and tastier. And the rabbit is for your dinner, because it is a light and tender snack, so you will be able to sleep well afterward."

The lion smiled and rested his paw on the fox's shoulder. "You are so fair, Little Fox. Where did you learn such behavior?"

"Oh, Your Majesty, Mr. Lion, I shall tell you, but you must promise that you will not become angry."

"Tell me."

"Do you promise not to hurt me?"

"I promise."

"I learned from watching your anger at the wolf."

The lion laughed out loud. "Take everything, Fox. You deserve it for being so smart." And he left the bull, the deer, and the rabbit with the fox and disappeared into the forest, still chuckling to himself.

The Wise Man and the Scorpion

20

A wise old man, whose name was Kumiel, sat pondering on the banks of the Euphrates. The sunbeams danced on the clear water of the river, and Kumiel gazed at the tall date palms, the pomegranate trees, and the grapevines as they cast their shadows on the water and the riverbank. Kumiel was thirsty and he stood up to take a drink from the river.

Then he spotted a scorpion that had fallen into the river. The creature could only just keep itself afloat.

The wise Kumiel looked at the poor scorpion and decided to save it. He held out his hand to pick it up, but at that moment the scorpion stung him.

Kumiel screamed. Waving his hand in the air, he began to spin around in pain. His white djellaba danced around him.

A little later, when the pain had worn off, Kumiel walked back to the river. The scorpion was still there, struggling with all its might to reach the riverbank. But scorpions are unable to swim. Kumiel decided to try once again to rescue the creature, so he reached out his hand—and was stung for a second time.

"Ow!" shrieked the wise Kumiel. He leaped up and began to dance with pain again.

But, before long, Kumiel reached out his hand to the half-drowned scorpion for the third time—and yet again the scorpion stung his hand.

And the same thing happened over and over again.

Another man, who had been fishing nearby, came to see what Kumiel was shouting about. He looked in surprise at the old man in his white djellaba, who was trying to save the scorpion over and over again and being stung over and over again.

"Hey, wise Kumiel, what on earth are you doing? Why did you not learn your lesson the first time? Or the second? Or the third? You're doing your best to save that creature, and instead of thanks, you get stung. You should give up!"

The wise Kumiel did not listen to the man.

He went on trying to rescue the scorpion—until finally he succeeded.

Kumiel, as quick as a flash, put the scorpion on the ground. The creature scuttled off and disappeared into the bushes.

Kumiel walked over to the fisherman and tapped him on the shoulder. "So you want to know why I did it, my dear friend? It is in the scorpion's nature to sting. And it is in my nature to help. Why should I let his nature win, and not mine?"

The fisherman headed home, feeling that he had learned something important that day. Kumiel went home too, because he was tired, and he needed herbal salve for his hand. And the scorpion? It sat there in the bushes for days, recovering from its fright, before leaving the river, never to return. 🪲

Rodaan Al Galidi

Rodaan Al Galidi was born in the south of Iraq. In 1998, he went to the Netherlands and lived in an asylum seekers' center for nine years. He was not allowed to work at the time, but he could write—and, luckily, he has continued to do so ever since. Writing in Dutch, he is the author of several award-winning collections of poetry and novels. In 2011, he received the European Union Prize for Literature. *The Three Princes of Serendip* is his first book for children (and secretly for grown-ups too).

Geertje Aalders

Geertje Aalders is an illustrator and a master in the art of cutting paper. She created all the pictures in this book with her knife, a pair of scissors, and lots and lots of colored paper. She also paints and draws and is inspired by the countryside, where she collects dead beetles and frogs and takes photographs of strange plants and old twisted trees. She lives in the Netherlands.

Laura Watkinson

Laura Watkinson's award-winning translations include *The Letter for the King* by Tonke Dragt and *Winter in Wartime* by Jan Terlouw. She lives in a tall, thin house on a canal in Amsterdam with her husband and three cats.

This book is for my best friends, Yem and Bender.
I hope they will give this book to their best friends
and that those best friends will give it to their
own best friends, so that eventually the whole
world will become best friends with one another.
RAG

For Janne and Floris
GA

Text copyright © 2017 by Rodaan Al Galidi
Illustrations copyright © 2017 by Geertje Aalders
Translation copyright © 2021 by Laura Watkinson

First US edition 2021
First published by Gottmer Publishing Group (Netherlands) 2017

Library of Congress Catalog Card Number pending
ISBN 978-1-5362-1450-5

APS 26 25 24 23 22 21
10 9 8 7 6 5 4 3 2 1

Printed in Humen, Dongguan, China

This book was typeset in Superclarendon.
The illustrations were done in cut paper.

Candlewick Press
99 Dover Street
Somerville, Massachusetts 02144

www.candlewick.com